When I'm Feeling
ANGRY

Written and illustrated by Trace Moroney

The Five Mile Press

When I'm feeling angry
I feel like there is a
boiling hot volcano in my tummy
that is about to . . .

explo

When I'm feeling angry
I want to kick and scream and

stomp . . .

stomp . . .

stomp my feet so hard
that the whole world shakes.

I want to run and run, and never stop.

Everyone gets angry sometimes.

Some things just make me
so mad . . . like when
someone
makes fun
of me . . .

or when someone ruins my sandcastle . . .

or when I get blamed for something
I didn't do.

Feeling angry isn't wrong.

But letting my anger hurt someone else is.

When I'm feeling angry I try to remember
to do the things that make me feel better . . .

like taking great big breaths . . .
in . . . and . . . out

or
going
to
my
favourite
quiet
place.

Talking about *why* I'm feeling angry,
with someone who cares about me,
can help make some of the anger go away.

And, sometimes, I get *soooo* angry
that I forget what it was
that made me angry in the first place . . .

and *that*
makes
me
laugh!

Background Notes for Parents

Self-esteem is the key

The greatest gift you can give your child is healthy self-esteem. Children who *feel valuable,* and who *trust themselves* have positive self-esteem. You can help your child *feel valuable* by spending quality time with him or her, playing games, reading books, or just listening. You can also help children *feel valuable* by helping them discover and become the person they want to be. Success follows people who genuinely *like who they are.*

However, happiness is more than just being successful. Helping your child gain the *self-trust* needed to deal with failure, loss, shame, difficulty and defeat is as important – if not more so – than succeeding or being best. When children trust themselves to handle painful feelings – fear, anger and sadness – they gain an *inner* security that allows them to embrace the world in which they live.

Each of these *FEELINGS* books has been carefully designed to help children better understand their feelings, and in doing so, gain greater autonomy (freedom) over their lives. Talking about feelings teaches children that it is normal to feel sad, or angry, or scared at times. With greater tolerance of painful feelings, children become free to enjoy their world, to feel secure in their abilities, and to be happy.

Feeling ANGRY

Healthy self-esteem reduces defensiveness and anger. Anger is one of the most difficult emotions to come to terms with. Children need to know that everyone gets angry sometimes, and that it's a natural feeling. By giving children the chance to put their side of the story, they not only *feel valued* but get to vent their anger in a healthy way. By helping children find their own solution, and then to act on it, they build the *self-trust* needed to have angry feelings but not be controlled by them.

Written by psychologists Bill Hallam and Dr Craig Olsson

For my sister, Sarah

Visit Trace Moroney at www.tracemoroney.com

The Five Mile Press Pty Ltd
1 Centre Road, Scoresby
Victoria 3179 Australia
www.fivemile.com.au

First published 2005

National Library of Australia Cataloguing-in-Publication data
Moroney, Trace
When I'm feeling angry.

For children
ISBN 978 1 74124 543 1 (paperback)

I. Title

A823.3

Printed in China 11 10 9 8